OPIOIDS AND OPIATES:
THE SILENT EPIDEMIC

The Heroin Crisis

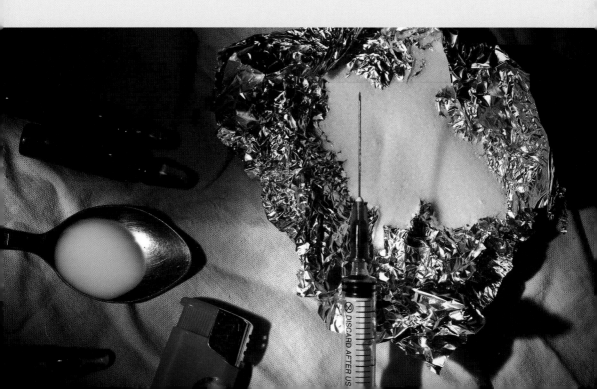

YOU ARE NOT ALONE

OPIOIDS AND OPIATES:
THE SILENT EPIDEMIC

Chronic Pain and Prescription Painkillers
The Dangers of Drug Abuse
The Heroin Crisis
Preventing and Treating Addiction
Who Is Using Opioids and Opiates?

OPIOIDS AND OPIATES:
THE SILENT EPIDEMIC

The Heroin Crisis

JOHN CASHIN

MASON CREST
PHILADELPHIA

Mason Crest
450 Parkway Drive, Suite D
Broomall, PA 19008
www.masoncrest.com

©2018 by Mason Crest, an imprint of National Highlights, Inc.

Printed and bound in the United States of America.

CPSIA Compliance Information: Batch #OPO2017.
For further information, contact Mason Crest at 1-866-MCP-Book.

First printing
1 3 5 7 9 8 6 4 2

Library of Congress Cataloging-in-Publication Data

on file at the Library of Congress
ISBN: 978-1-4222-3825-7 (hc)
ISBN: 978-1-4222-7965-6 (ebook)

OPIOIDS AND OPIATES: THE SILENT EPIDEMIC series ISBN: 978-1-4222-3822-6

QR CODES AND LINKS TO THIRD-PARTY CONTENT

Table of Contents

KEY ICONS TO LOOK FOR:

Words to understand: These words with their easy-to-understand definitions will increase the reader's understanding of the text while building vocabulary skills.

Sidebars: This boxed material within the main text allows readers to build knowledge, gain insights, explore possibilities, and broaden their perspectives by weaving together additional information to provide realistic and holistic perspectives.

Educational Videos: Readers can view videos by scanning our QR codes, providing them with additional educational content to supplement the text. Examples include news coverage, moments in history, speeches, iconic sports moments and much more!

Text-dependent questions: These questions send the reader back to the text for more careful attention to the evidence presented there.

Research projects: Readers are pointed toward areas of further inquiry connected to each chapter. Suggestions are provided for projects that encourage deeper research and analysis.

Series glossary of key terms: This back-of-the book glossary contains terminology used throughout this series. Words found here increase the reader's ability to read and comprehend higher-level books and articles in this field.

 Words to Understand in This Chapter

narcotic—a drug that in small doses dulls the senses, relieves pain, and
　　induces sleep, but in larger doses can depress breathing and heartbeat.

neurotransmitters—chemicals that are released at the end of a nerve and
　　carry messages to other parts of the body.

synaptic cleft—a microscopic gap between neurons. The nervous system
　　uses neurotransmitters to send messages across this gap.

synthetic—a substance that is created in a laboratory by blending chemicals.
　　Synthetic substances often imitate a natural product.

withdrawal—a syndrome of physical and emotional symptoms that a person
　　addicted to heroin or opioids experiences when the person stops using
　　the drug.

Heroin is an illegal drug that is often sold as a refined brown or white powder. At one time, heroin was generally considered one of the most hardcore drugs. However, in recent years the street price of heroin has dropped while the purity has increased, making it more appealing to young recreational drug users.

A Growing Crisis

Since the year 2000, more than 500,000 Americans have died from drug overdoses. More than 60 percent of these deaths involved a class of *narcotic* drugs called opioids. The opioids include illegal drugs like heroin, as well as other drugs that are legally prescribed as painkillers, such as oxycodone, hydrocodone, codeine, and fentanyl, among others.

Public health officials agree that the United States is facing a major crisis when it comes to heroin and other opioids. According to 2017 data from the Centers for Disease Control (CDC), heroin-related overdose deaths more than tripled between 2010 and 2015. In both 2015 and 2016, approximately 13,000 Americans died from heroin overdoses.

The CDC also found that the rate of overdose death related to other opioids has increased greatly over the past few years.

A bag of fentanyl pills seized in a DEA raid. Because Fentanyl causes effects similar to heroin, it is sometimes blended with low-grade heroin to make it more potent.

From 2014 to 2015, the number of deaths involving *synthetic* opioids rose by more than 72 percent, to nearly 10,000 deaths a year. One opioid in particular, fentanyl, is credited by the CDC for driving up the death rate. Fentanyl can be fifty to one hundred times more potent than heroin sold on the streets.

How Does Heroin Work?

Heroin and other opioids work by affecting the user's brain and central nervous system. The cells of the nervous system, called neurons, that transmit directions from the brain to different parts of the body. There are approximately 100 billion neurons in the brain alone. However, the neurons do not actually touch each other. Neurons are separated by a gap, called a synapse or *synaptic cleft.*

For messages to cross the synapse, the neuron must release a chemical called a *neurotransmitter*, which crosses this space to the adjacent neuron. The neurotransmitter binds to a special port on the surface of the neuron, which is called a receptor. Each receptor on a neuron can recognize a specific neurotransmitter—the two of them fit together. In a way, this is like the charging cable for a digital device. If you don't have the right type of plug, it won't connect. The same thing is true for neurotransmitters and receptors. They need to be the right "match" or they won't be able to recognize each other and take the next step. When a neurotransmitter binds to a receptor, it will either produce an effect or it will inhibit an effect in the neuron.

When opioids enter the brain, the neurons mistakenly think they are neurotransmitters because they fit into certain receptors. The drugs overwhelm the neurons in the brain, producing effects that are similar to (but stronger than) those produced by the neurotransmitters endorphin and enkephalin. Heroin also binds to receptors on neurons in the brain stem,

 Educational Video

Scan here to see how opioid drugs interact with receptors in the brain and nervous system:

which controls important processes, such as blood pressure and breathing. As a result, the effects of heroin include:

- increased analgesia, or reduction of pain sensations;
- feelings of pleasure, relaxation, and decreased alertness; and
- slowed respiration (breathing) and heartbeat.

The effects of heroin depend on several factors. These include how much of the drug a person takes, and the way in which the drug is administered. Heroin acts faster, and its effects are stronger, when it is injected. If the user sniffs ("snorts") a powdered version of the drug or inhales vapors after heating or smoking heroin, the drug takes longer to reach the brain and its effects are weaker.

The synthetic opioid fentanyl tends to depress a person's respiration much more than heroin. This increases the risk of an accidental overdose. Sometimes, fentanyl is added to low-quality heroin to increase its potency. In other cases, a person

 Did You Know?

Scientists have found three types of opioid receptors on the nerve cells. They are named after letters in the Greek alphabet—mu, delta, and kappa receptors. Each of these receptors plays a different role. For example, mu receptors are responsible for opioids' pleasurable effects and their ability to relieve pain.

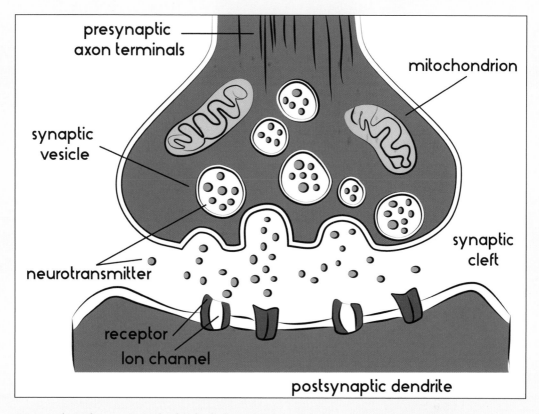

presynaptic axon terminals

mitochondrion

synaptic vesicle

neurotransmitter

synaptic cleft

receptor

Ion channel

postsynaptic dendrite

Drugs alter the way people think, feel, and behave by disrupting communication between nerve cells (neurons) in the brain. Neurons are separated by small spaces called synapses. Messages are passed from cell to cell across the synapse by specialized molecules, called neurotransmitters, which bind to receptors on the nerve cells. Prescription opioids and heroin produce effects that are similar to—but stronger than—those produced by the neurotransmitters endorphin and enkephalin: reduced pain, decreased alertness, and slowed respiration.

may think they are buying heroin when they are actually receiving pure fentanyl. If a person who is used to shooting up a certain quantity of heroin takes the same-size dose of fentanyl, death from overdose is nearly certain.

Another side effect of opioids like heroin and fentanyl is that people who use these drugs regularly develop a physical dependence on them. As a user's nervous system becomes used to regular doses of the drug, it stops naturally producing the neurotransmitters. This means the user must take larger amounts of the drug in order to achieve the same euphoric effects. In addition, if the user tries to stop using an opioid he or she will suffer from unpleasant physical effects, known as *withdrawal*. These generally include severe headaches, uncontrolled trembling, chills, pain and muscle spasms, insomnia, diarrhea, and vomiting. Some people experience nightmares, hallucinations, and depression. The symptoms of withdrawal can last for several weeks, and most addicts will do nearly anything to avoid them.

Causes of the Crisis

The present heroin crisis has been fueled by two important developments. One of them was the recognition by law enforcement officials and medical practitioners that there was a growing problem with abuse of opioid painkillers. Doctors began to reduce the number of prescriptions they wrote for opioids, and police began to crack down on illegal operations that sold the painkillers. But reducing the supply of opioid painkillers meant that patients who had become addicted to the drugs had to find other ways to get high.

The second important development was the greater availability of illegal heroin on the streets of cities and towns throughout the United States. Although the U.S. government has been waging a "war on drugs" since the 1960s, it has been unable to prevent illegal drugs from being smuggled over the borders. This is largely due to the rise of well-organized and well-financed drug selling operations, often referred to in the media as *drug cartels*.

Since 2005, drug cartels in Mexico have increased the amount of heroin that they produce each year, and have also increased the purity of the drugs. As a result, the American black market has been flooded with a supply of cheap, pure heroin. Consequently, heroin became an inexpensive substitute for people who were addicted to painkillers but could no longer get prescriptions for them. At the same time, growing numbers of young people are trying heroin and becoming addicted.

 Text-Dependent Questions

1. Approximately how many Americans die annually due to heroin overdoses?
2. What synthetic opioid is credited with driving up the overdose death rate?
3. What factors affect how strongly the effects of heroin are felt by users?

 Research Project

The National Center for Health Statistics at the Centers for Disease Control and Prevention does collect information on many of the more commonly used drugs. Visit their website:

www.drugabuse.gov/related-topics/trends-statistics/overdose-death-rates

and find information about the number of heroin and opioid overdose deaths each year since 2002. Using this data, create a bar chart. Share the information with your class.

 Words to Understand in This Chapter

demographics—statistical data relating to the population and particular groups within it.

impurity—something that contaminates or taints a product.

laudanum—a solution that contains alcohol and opium, which was used as a painkiller from the fifteenth to the nineteenth centuries.

prevalence—the degree or rate at which something happens.

synthesize—to create something by combining elements or chemicals into a single solution.

Sap drips from the seed pod of an opium poppy. When collected and dried, this sap is known as opium. The Latin name for the opium poppy, **Papaver somniferum** *means "sleep-bringing poppy," referring to the sedative properties of opium and the drugs derived from it, such as morphine and heroin.*

A Short History of Heroin

Humans have been aware of the euphoria-producing effects of the opium poppy for roughly 5,000 years. The people of ancient Sumeria, in Mesopotamia (modern-day Iraq) grew poppy plants and extracted juice from them to use in religious rituals and as medicine. The Sumerians called the poppy plant *hul gil*, or the "joy plant." The people of the Minoan civilization on the island of Crete also processed poppy juice into a substance that they called *ópion* around 2500 BCE. (The modern word *opium* is a Latin version of the Greek *ópion*.)

Opium would become a widely used drug in the major civilizations of the ancient world. It was widely used in Egypt, as well as in the Persian, Greek, and Roman empires. Arab traders

Ethnic Chinese smoke opium in a small room, 1924. Such opium dens were popular on the West Coast of the United States and Canada during the mid-nineteenth century, due to the influx of Chinese immigrants prior to the 1880s. After 1885 the US government cracked down on the recreational use of opium and also restricted immigration from Asia.

spread the drug to many new lands, including China and southeast Asia, by the ninth century CE.

Easing Pain

During the sixteenth and seventeenth centuries, European doctors began to use an opium solution they called *laudanum* as a painkiller, as well as to relieve other medical problems. Opium was also popular as a recreational drug, used by many famous people including the poet Samuel Taylor Coleridge, British naval hero Lord Horatio Nelson, and even American leaders like Thomas Jefferson and Benjamin Franklin. Those who regularly took the drug were known in the eighteenth and nineteenth centuries as "opium-eaters."

In 1804, a German chemist named Friedrich Sertürner isolated another drug from opium, which he called morphine. It was more effective at reducing pain than opium. But morphine was also even more addictive than opium. It was widely used as a painkiller during the American Civil War (1861–65), but addiction to the drug became so common it was referred to as "the soldiers' disease."

Scientists continued looking for a painkiller that was not so addictive. In the late 1890s, Felix Hoffman, a chemist working for the Bayer drug company in Germany, *synthesized* a compound from morphine that was even more effective as a painkiller. He called this new drug heroin, because he said that it would have "heroic" qualities in medicine. Heroin was prescribed for many conditions—a liquid version was even used as a cough syrup for children! However, doctors, as well as the government, soon realized that the drug was even more addictive than morphine or opium.

 Educational Video

Scan here to see a video with personal stories from heroin addicts and their loved ones.

Heroin Restrictions

In the United States, the Pure Food and Drug Act of 1906 restricted the use of opium or heroin in patent medicines. The 1914 Harrison Narcotics Tax Act further restricted the sale of opiates, as well as some other drugs.

By the 1920s, other opioids that could replace heroin and morphine were being synthesized in laboratories. These included oxycodone (1916), hydrocodone (1920), and hydromorphone (1924). Methadone was created in 1937. By the end of the Second World War in 1945, heroin addiction was at one-tenth of the level it had been twenty years earlier.

However, recreational use of opiates gradually increased again in the decades after the Second World War. During the 1960s, U.S. soldiers stationed in Vietnam or Southeast Asia were often exposed to heroin; many came home addicted to the

 Did You Know?

As the United States began to crack down on the recreational use of heroin and other opiates in the 1910s and 1920s, there were many people who were addicted to opiates and could no longer get the drugs legally. Some of them sought to continue buying the drugs through illegal sources, so they would not have to suffer from withdrawal symptoms. In New York City during the 1920s there were a group of addicts who made a living by salvaging scrap metal from local garbage dumps. They were nicknamed "junkies." Today, that term is often used to refer to heroin addicts.

Federal narcotics agents shovel confiscated blocks of heroin into an incinerator, 1936.

drug. The number of heroin addicts in the U.S. increased throughout the decade. Despite some high-profile overdose deaths—including the rock stars Janis Joplin (1970) and Jim Morrison (1971)—the number of heroin users continued to rise.

Controlling Drugs

In response to the growing problems of recreational drug use and heroin addiction, the U.S. government passed the

Controlled Substances Act of 1970. This law created five "schedules," or categories, of drugs, and established penalties that include heavy fines and imprisonment for the illegal sale or use of drugs. All pharmeceuticals—from ordinary prescription drugs to dangerous narcotics—are included on one of the following schedules:

- Schedule I controlled substances are considered to have no accepted medical use while also having a high potential for abuse. Heroin is a schedule I drug, and so are ecstasy, LSD, and marijuana.
- Substances on schedules II or III can be prescribed to treat medical conditions, but they are also considered to have a relatively high potential for abuse or addiction. Schedule II includes opioids like morphine, codeine, fentanyl, and oxycodone, as well as stimulants like amphetamines and methamphetamine diet pills. Cocaine, which is sometimes used for certain medical procedures, is a schedule II drug.
- Schedule III includes some products that contain several different drugs, such as Tylenol with codeine, as well as anabolic steroids.
- Schedules IV and V include drugs that have a medicinal purpose and a relatively low potential for abuse or addiction. Schedule IV drugs include sleep aids like Xanax, anti-anxiety drugs like Valium, and muscle relaxants like Klonopin. Schedule V drugs include some types of cough syrup that contain several controlled substances.

Since passage of the Controlled Substances Act, the federal and state governments have passed many other laws that make it illegal to possess, manufacture, or sell heroin and other drugs. In 1973 the U.S. government created the Drug Enforcement Agency to help limit the availability of heroin and other illegal opiates.

Increasing Use

During the 1970s and 1980s, heroin was ostracized as a "hard drug"—a drug that only hardcore drug abusers would take, unlike drugs like marijuana and even cocaine, which were viewed as more recreational drugs. Heroin users were viewed as "junkies" who were losers and criminals. The way that heroin users got high probably had something to do with attitudes toward the drug. Users typically injected a liquid heroin solution into a vein. This made the user susceptible to contracting diseases like HIV or hepatitis from shared needles. There was also the danger of accidental overdose.

During the mid-1990s, the heroin sold on the streets in the United States reached very high levels of purity. This meant that it was possible for a user to take heroin in other ways, such as smoking or snorting the powder. As a result, negative attitudes toward heroin use began to soften. As a result, the number of people willing to try heroin increased.

Historically, the number of adolescents who use heroin in the United States has been low. The *Monitoring the Future* survey conducted annually by the National Institute on Drug Abuse found that from 1979 to 1994, about 0.5 percent of high-school seniors used heroin. However, the rate began to climb in

Heroin is produced from the resin of the opium poppy. It often comes as a white or brown powder (top) that can be snorted, smoked, or injected in solution into the bloodstream with a needle. Black tar heroin (right) is not as highly processed as other forms of heroin, and contains many impurities as a result.

the mid-1990s. By the year 2000, 2.1 percent of high-school students had used heroin during the previous year, a significant increase. The annual *prevalence* of heroin use among high-school students stabilized at around 1.5 percent during the decade from 2000 to 2010, then began to fall. This was probably due in part to better education about the dangers of heroin. By 2016, the annual prevalence rate of heroin use among high-school seniors had dropped back to 0.6 percent.

Although the rate of heroin use among American adolescents has fallen back to its historic level, the rate of heroin use continues to rise among all other age groups. A 2016 study by the Centers for Disease Control (CDC) found that among young adults aged eighteen to twenty-five, the rate of heroin use has more than doubled since 2004, rising from 3.5 percent to 7.3 percent. The heroin use rate increased by 58 percent among adults over the age of 26, rising from 1.2 percent to approximately 2 percent of this population.

The CDC study found that some of the greatest increases in heroin use occurred in *demographic* groups with historically low rates of heroin use. For example, the prevalence of heroin use doubled among women over the past decade, with the rate rising from 0.8 percent to 1.6 percent. Among men, the use rate rose from 2.4 percent to 3.6 percent, a 50 percent increase in that same period.

Economic data indicates that heroin use has increased by over 60 percent among people of all income levels over the past

 Did You Know?

The increase in purity of heroin is due in part to the Latin American drug cartels. As these organizations grew larger, they began to employ chemists who could improve the ways that they processed drugs like heroin and cocaine, or could make the popular illegal drug methamphetamine. These cartel chemists turned their attention to refining the traditional black tar heroin produced in Mexico. They developed processes by which Mexican heroin could be made almost twice as pure as the old black tar product. This Mexican powder product was much more appealing to American customers.

decade. The CDC study found that the rate of heroin use rose from 3.4 percent to 5.5 percent among people making less than $20,000 a year. It rose from 1.3 percent to 2.3 percent among those making $20,000 to $49,999 a year. And it increased from 1 percent to 1.6 percent among those making $50,000 or more annually. A similar 60 percent increase was seen whether the person had no health insurance coverage, was covered under a government program such as Medicaid, or received health insurance coverage from an employer or other source.

Street Heroin

In the United States, illegal heroin is commonly found in one of three varieties. "Black tar" heroin is found primarily in the western and southern states. It looks like a black sticky paste. This form of the drug is not as processed as other forms, and often contains many *impurities*. Historically, black tar heroin was the most common form of the drug that was smuggled from Mexico or Latin America. Because of the impurities, black tar heroin is usually injected, rather than being snorted or smoked.

In the 1990s, Mexican and Colombian drug cartels began to produce more refined forms of heroin. As a result, Mexican heroin began to be sold as a brownish powder. Because of additional processing, the powder was pure enough that it could be smoked or inhaled. This made it more attractive as a drug to younger, less experienced drug users, who preferred not to inject drugs.

A white powdered form of heroin was historically found primarily on the East Coast of the United States. This heroin is also very pure, and generally originated in Southeast Asia. However, recent reports from the DEA indicate that Mexican drug cartels are now producing white-powder heroin from poppies grown in Mexico.

In all cases, the form of heroin that an addict buys is rarely ever pure heroin. Drug dealers often mix (or "cut") their product with other drugs, such as fentanyl, to make it more potent, or with other powdery substances, such as sugar or baking soda, to change the color or increase the quantity. This can make buyers believe they are getting more for their money.

 Text-Dependent Questions

1. What German chemist first synthesized heroin?
2. What did the Controlled Substances Act of 1970 create?
3. What are the three most common forms of heroin?

 Research Project

What does the opioid addiction problem look like in your local community? For this research project, you will research what is happening. Three sources of information are necessary. These can be articles from the local or state newspapers, news videos about the problem, statements from law enforcement and medical personnel, even interviews with your school administrators or counselors. Ask: is opioid abuse a problem here? How has drug addiction changed over the last few years? What is being done to educate people about drugs?

When you are finished, write a one-page essay about what you found. Be sure to list your sources at the end of your essay.

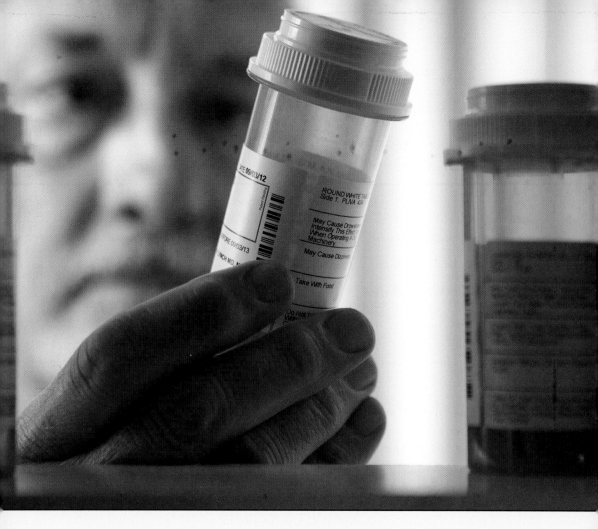

 Words to Understand in This Chapter

chronic pain—pain that lasts for at least three to six months consecutively, or is present for three to six non-consecutive months during a twelve-month period.

pill mill—illegal medical clinics or pharmacies in which doctors or pharmacists prescribe or supply opioids without a legitimate medical reason.

vested interest—when someone wants something to happen in a certain way because it will benefit them.

Despite the rising number of deaths directly linked to opioids, these drugs continue to be routinely prescribed to people suffering from chronic pain. The pharmaceutical industry makes billions of dollars each year from prescription opioids such as oxycodone and hydrocodone. More than 200 million prescriptions for opioid pain relievers are filled each year in the United States, with another 20 million opioid prescriptions dispensed in Canada annually.

The Pill Problem

A key element of the current heroin crisis has to do with another sort of drug—opioid painkillers. These started to be prescribed in growing amounts during the late 1990s. Opioid painkillers were thought to be a good solution to the problem of *chronic pain*.

Chronic pain is defined as pain that lasts for at least three to six months consecutively, or is present for three to six nonconsecutive months during a twelve-month period. Sometimes, chronic pain can be traced to an injury. It could also be the result of a medical condition, such as arthritis, multiple sclerosis, or cancer. Migraine headaches and low back pain also qualify as chronic pain. The American Pain Society recently report-

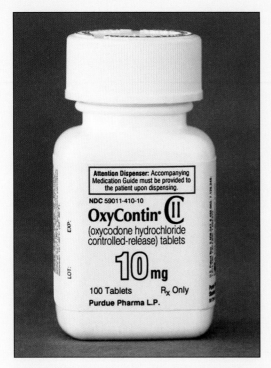

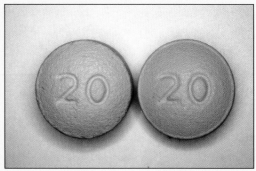

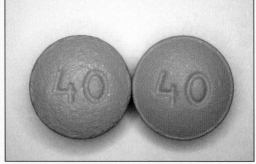

OxyContin is a popular brand of opioid painkiller in which the drug is slowly released into the person's system over a twelve-hour period. It comes in strengths ranging from 10 to 80 milligrams; pictured (above, right) are 20 and 40 milligram doses.

ed that nearly 50 million adults in the United States suffer from chronic pain or severe pain.

Doctors often prescribe painkilling medications to help people deal with chronic pain. Opioid pain relievers are by far the most common form of prescription pain medication. This type of medication is used because it is very effective in treating pain and relieving discomfort.

However, opioid painkillers are also highly addictive and can be dangerous. According to the Centers for Disease Control and Prevention (CDC), each year at least half of all opioid overdoses in the United States involve a prescription opioid. Since 1999, more than 200,000 Americans have died from overdoses of prescription opioids.

Pharmaceutical Companies Drive a Crisis

By the 1990s, pain societies began encouraging doctors to push for the increased use of opioids for all types of pain, including non-cancer pain. According to the American Association of Retired Persons, this push for more extensive use of painkillers was largely financed by pharmaceutical companies who had a *vested interest* in making a profit. The drug makers greatly downplayed the medications' potential for addiction while exaggerating their effectiveness. As a result, physicians had the impression that prescription painkillers were much safer and more effective for chronic pain than they truly were.

 Did You Know?

Most people obtain painkillers via a prescription. Studies show that 18 percent of people who abuse prescription painkillers got them from the same physician. And another 54.2 percent received the painkillers for free from a relative or friend—who obtained the drugs from a single physician in 81.6 percent of all cases. Abusers use various methods to escape detection, such as "doctor shopping," in which they obtain prescriptions from different doctors to get large amounts or regular refills of the drug.

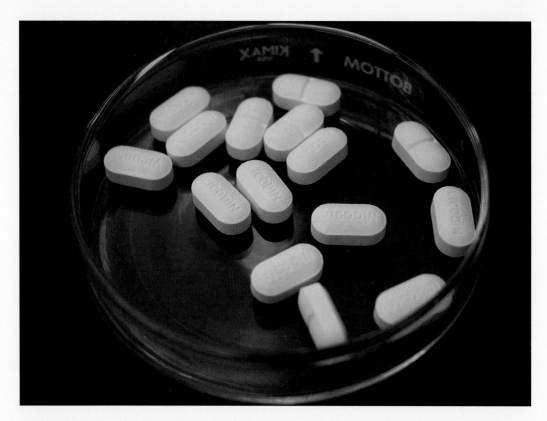

Hydrocodone is an opioid pain medication. These pills were sold under the trade name Vicodin.

Between 1996 and 2002, Purdue Pharma, the manufacturer of OxyContin (a brand name for oxycodone), financed over 20,000 educational programs for physicians. Many of these programs endorsed the long-term use of opioids for chronic pain. The campaigns were successful. Over the next 15 years, opioid pain reliever use in the United States doubled and oxycodone use grew almost fivefold. Purdue's heavy marketing of the drug resulted in people across North America using it for all types of pain, including toothaches and back pain.

However, researchers found hardly any evidence to support the claim that long-term opioid use helps with chronic pain. Instead, they discovered overwhelming evidence pointing to the potential for abuse, addiction, overdose, falls, fractures, constipation, sexual dysfunction, and heart attacks. In 2007, Purdue Pharma pleaded guilty to criminal charges for misrepresenting the dangers of its product, and agreed to pay over $600 million in fines. Despite this, other pharmaceutical companies soon got into the lucrative opioid painkiller business.

Pill Mills and Untrained Physicians

Although most physicians prescribe painkillers in a genuine attempt to prevent abuse and addiction, a few rogue physicians have contributed to the opioid crisis. Unscrupulous doctors have strong financial incentive for supplying prescription painkillers out of their office. They can buy opioids wholesale, repackage them, and sell them to patients at a much higher price, with profits ranging from 60 to 300 percent. These illegal operations in which doctors, clinics, or pharmacists prescribe or supply opioids without a legitimate medical reason are called *pill mills*.

 Educational Video

To see a video of drug enforcement agents arresting a pill mill doctor, scan here:

Newspaper headlines announce the death of the pop star Prince in April 2016. The talented musician overdosed on fentanyl, an opioid painkiller that he had been prescribed to treat a hip injury.

In recent years the federal government has taken steps to identify and shut down pill mills. A major bust occurred in May of 2015, when the DEA arrested about 280 people, including 22 doctors and pharmacists who were dispensing opioids in Arkansas, Louisiana, Mississippi and Alabama. The DEA has also provided guidelines to pharmaceutical companies intended to help them identify operations that might be pill mills. The drug companies are now required to let federal officials know if they identify any suspicious activity.

The new rules did not have a meaningful effect on the number of opioid painkiller prescriptions. The number of pills prescribed annually in the United States has remained around 200 million, with about 31 million prescribed in Canada each year. However, the changes did make it harder for some addicted people to get the drug. This led to an unexpected consequence—prescription drug users began turning to an illegal drug, heroin, to satisfy their cravings. And ruthless criminal organizations based in Mexico and elsewhere were more than happy to provide the drugs.

 Text-Dependent Questions

1. What is chronic pain?
2. Why did pain societies begin encouraging doctors to prescribe opioids for all types of pain during the 1990s?
3. What is a "pill mill?"

 Research Project

Research whether your state or province has a prescription drug monitoring program. Write a one-page summary of rules surrounding the program—such as who manages the program, who can access the program, and the information that the program provides. If your state or province does not have a PDMP, share your beliefs in support or against the creation of a PDMP in your area.

Words to Understand in This Chapter

drug trafficking organizations (DTOs)—complex organizations with highly defined command-and-control structures that produce, transport, and/or distribute large quantities of one or more illicit drugs. This is an official term used by the federal government to describe drug cartels.

law of supply and demand—an economic theory that explains the interaction between the supply of a resource and the demand for that resource. Generally, if there is not much of a product but there is a high demand for it, the price will increase. If there is a large supply but a low demand, the price tends to fall.

4

Drug Cartels and Heroin

A *cartel* is an association of businesses that agree to work together in order to set the price for a commodity or service that they control. One well-known example of a legitimate cartel is OPEC, an international association of countries that possess significant oil reserves. OPEC affects the global price of oil by regulating the amount of oil that its members produce each year. The DeBeers group of companies is another cartel that for many years dominated the production and sale of diamonds worldwide.

The term *drug cartels* originated in the 1980s, when some of the major cocaine dealers in Colombia agreed to work together on production and distribution of that drug. Today, the term *drug cartels* is popularly used to refer to any criminal organization that makes its money primarily from manufacturing, smuggling and distributing illegal drugs. In official reports the DEA, FBI, and other agencies often refer to drug cartels as *drug trafficking organizations*, or DTOs.

Since the mid-1990s, drug cartels from Mexico have dominated the global trade in illegal drugs. The Mexican cartels, such as the notorious Sinaloa Cartel, operate like international corporations—they make partnerships with street gangs and crime organizations in the United States and other countries in order to distribute drugs. As a result, the Sinaloa Cartel earns an estimated $20 billion a year in profits from its drug smuggling and selling operations.

Waging a War on Drugs

Since the 1970s, the U.S. government has passed many laws intended to prevent the flow of drugs into the country and to bring down drug dealers. In addition, every year the U.S. Congress provides roughly $3 billion in funding that the Drug Enforcement Administration (DEA) uses to try to prevent illegal drugs from being smuggled into the United States. Other federal agencies, such as the U.S. Border Patrol, the Federal Bureau of Investigation (FBI), and the U.S. Coast Guard, also devote significant resources to stopping drug smugglers. State and municipal governments spend billions each year on their own efforts to break up drug rings and imprison drug dealers in their communities. In all, experts estimate that the United States spends more than $25 billion every year on anti-drug efforts.

However, the money that cartels make from drug sales is far greater than what the U.S. spends to prevent them. In

Federal Drug Trafficking Penalties

Federal Trafficking Penalties for Schedules I, II, III, IV, and V (except Marijuana)

Schedule	Substance/Quantity	Penalty	Substance/Quantity	Penalty
II	Cocaine 500-4999 grams mixture	**First Offense:** Not less than 5 yrs. and not more than 40 yrs. If death or serious bodily injury, not less than 20 yrs. or more than life. Fine of not more than $5 million if an individual, $25 million if not an individual. **Second Offense:** Not less than 10 yrs. and not more than life. If death or serious bodily injury, life imprisonment. Fine of not more than $8 million if an individual, $50 million if not an individual.	Cocaine 5 kilograms or more mixture	**First Offense:** Not less than 10 yrs. and not more than life. If death or serious bodily injury, not less than 20 yrs. or more than life. Fine of not more than $10 million if an individual, $50 million if not an individual. **Second Offense:** Not less than 20 yrs, and not more than life. If death or serious bodily injury, life imprisonment. Fine of not more than $20 million if an individual, $75 million if not an individual. **2 or More Prior Offenses:** Life imprisonment. Fine of not more than $20 million if an individual, $75 million if not an individual.
II	Cocaine Base 28-279 grams mixture		Cocaine Base 280 grams or more mixture	
IV	Fentanyl 40-399 grams mixture		Fentanyl 400 grams or more mixture	
I	Fentanyl Analogue 10-99 grams mixture		Fentanyl Analogue 100 grams or more mixture	
I	Heroin 100-999 grams mixture		Heroin 1 kilogram or more mixture	
I	LSD 1-9 grams mixture		LSD 10 grams or more mixture	
II	Methamphetamine 5-49 grams pure or 50-499 grams mixture		Methamphetamine 50 grams or more pure or 500 grams or more mixture	
II	PCP 10-99 grams pure or 100-999 grams mixture		PCP 100 grams or more pure or 1 kilogram or more mixture	

Substance/Quantity	Penalty
Any Amount Of Other Schedule I & II Substances Any Drug Product Containing Gamma Hydroxybutyric Acid Flunitrazepam (Schedule IV) 1 Gram	**First Offense**: Not more that 20 yrs. If death or serious bodily injury, not less than 20 yrs. or more than Life. Fine $1 million if an individual, $5 million if not an individual. **Second Offense:** Not more than 30 yrs. If death or serious bodily injury, life imprisonment. Fine $2 million if an individual, $10 million if not an individual.
Any Amount Of Other Schedule III Drugs	**First Offense**: Not more than 10 yrs. If death or serious bodily injury, not more that 15 yrs. Fine not more than $500,000 if an individual, $2.5 million if not an individual. **Second Offense**: Not more than 20 yrs. If death or serious injury, not more than 30 yrs. Fine not more than $1 million if an individual, $5 million if not an individual.
Any Amount Of All Other Schedule IV Drugs (other than one gram or more of Flunitrazepam)	**First Offense**: Not more than 5 yrs. Fine not more than $250,000 if an individual, $1 million if not an individual. **Second Offense**: Not more than 10 yrs. Fine not more than $500,000 if an individual, $2 million if other than an individual.
Any Amount Of All Schedule V Drugs	**First Offense**: Not more than 1 yr. Fine not more than $100,000 if an individual, $250,000 if not an individual. **Second Offense**: Not more than 4 yrs. Fine not more than $200,000 if an individual, $500,000 if not an individual.

This pile of cash, seized in a DEA raid on a heroin-selling operation, represents just a tiny fraction of the billions of dollars that drug cartels earn from the sale of their illegal products each year.

2016, Mexico's Secretary of Public Safety Genaro Garcia Luna claimed that Mexican drug cartels earn more than $64 billion from drug sales in the United States. Drug cartels based in other countries, such as Colombia, Russia, and China, work in much the same way, controlling their own shares of illegal drug markets in the United States, Canada, and other places.

The enormous amounts of money that the drug cartels can earn makes them willing to take risks and spend money to make sure their drug shipments can get into the United States.

The federal agencies responsible for preventing drug smuggling into the United States receive a lot of publicity when they announce the capture of a large drug shipment, or the breakup of a smuggling rung. However, the reality is that these high-profile "busts" hardly affect the operation, or the profits, of drug cartels. For every shipment that is captured, experts say, many more pass over the border undetected.

This fact can be proven by evaluating the effect of major drug busts on the street prices of drugs. When American police intercept a large shipment of heroin, this should cause the street price of heroin to rise. This is because of the economic law known as *supply and demand*—if the bust meant that less of the drug was available, the remaining supply of the drug could be sold for a higher price. What has actually happened, however, is that despite hundreds of highly publicized seizures, the street price of heroin in the United States is roughly half what it was twenty-five years ago. In 1992, according to DEA data, a gram of heroin cost about $250; in 2017, that gram of heroin cost about $110, with the price of a gram as low as $100 in some places. The prices of other drugs, such as marijuana and cocaine, are also lower now than they were two decades ago. The United States has been waging the Drug War since the 1970s, and it is losing.

Drug Smuggling from Mexico

Mexico has become the central network of the illegal drug trade because of its location between the United States and the major drug-producing countries of Central and South America. The FBI reports that more than 90 percent of the illegal drugs

A smuggling tunnel in Nogales. On the U.S. side of the border, the tunnel entrance (below) was hidden in the kitchen of a house owned by a leader of the Sinaloa drug cartel.

Educational Video

For a short film on abuse of heroin and prescription pills, scan here:

smuggled into the United States today come across the border from Mexico.

The U.S.-Mexico border is particularly vulnerable to drug smuggling because tens of thousands of people cross the border for legitimate business each day. Although Border Patrol agents attempt to carefully check every vehicle crossing from Mexico, smugglers have developed many creative hiding places in vehicles, making it extremely difficult to spot illegal drugs.

In addition, the border between the United States and Mexico stretches for nearly 2,000 miles, and passes through many remote, sparsely populated areas of desert. It is very challenging for U.S. and Mexican authorities to patrol this long border, and drug cartels take full advantage of any potential crossing point that is overlooked.

Smugglers also find creative ways to get drugs across the border. Since the mid-1990s Mexican drug traffickers have constructed more than a hundred tunnels connecting the city of Nogales, Arizona, with a city just over the border in Mexico that is also called Nogales. Some of the Nogales tunnels run for more than a half-mile underground. The tunnels often feature electric lighting and ventilation systems; one tunnel even had rails and a trolley system. The tunnel exits on the American side were generally located inside houses or businesses, so that drugs easily could be loaded into vehicles for transport to other parts of the United States. Dozens of other smuggling tunnels have also been found running between other American and Mexican cities.

Since 2006, US officials have constructed a controversial wall along the U.S.-Mexico border, in an effort to restrict smuggling and illegal immigration. During the 2016 presidential election, Donald Trump promised to build a new wall that would seal the border, and after his election his administration hired more Border Patrol guards. Drug cartels responded to increased efforts to prevent smuggling by land by using sea routes to avoid detection. Drugs can be carried on commercial cargo vessels, oil tankers, and small fishing boats. They are sometimes carried on small fiberglass speedboats, which are difficult to detect on radar and fast enough to evade Coast Guard vessels. Drug cartels have even built submersible diesel-powered crafts known as narco-submarines that can carry up to ten tons of heroin or other drugs into the United States undetected.

Drug Mules

Drug cartels use creative methods can be used to bring large quantities of drugs into the United States. However, most drugs enter the U.S. in much smaller quantities, carried by individual smugglers known as "drug mules." Many drug mules come into the United States on commercial flights, with drugs hidden in

Drug mules attempted to hide drugs inside the hidden compartment on the back of this flatbed truck. They were caught at a border crossing. For every mule that is caught, however, many others pass through safely. It is impossible for border patrol agents to thoroughly search every one of the more than 120 million vehicles that pass over the U.S.-Mexico border every year.

their luggage or under their clothing. Sometimes, the mule will hide the drugs inside their own bodies, swallowing latex balloons filled with heroin that can be excreted once they've arrived in the United States. This smuggling method can be very dangerous; if one of the containers bursts while inside a drug mule's stomach, that person is likely to die from the effects of ingesting such a large dose.

Some people don't even realize that they are drug mules. Drugs may be hidden in the suitcase or vehicle of an innocent

DEA agents escort Joaquín "El Chapo" Guzmán, the notorious head of the Sinaloa Cartel, to a court appearance in January 2017. Authorities believe Guzmán was responsible for the Sinaloa Cartel's decision to increase heroin production in the mid-2000. Guzmán was captured by Mexican authorities in 2016 and sent to the United States to stand trial.

person, and retrieved once the unsuspecting person has made it across the border.

At times, drug dealers may force people to become drug mules by threatening to hurt or kill members of their family if they do not smuggle the drugs successfully. However, it is more common for the drug cartels to employ poor people as drug mules. Carrying drugs offers an opportunity for the person to make much more money than they could ordinarily earn. Sometimes, drug addicts agree to carry illegal substances across the border in exchange for the drugs they crave. People of both sexes and all ages have served as drug mules.

In addition to paying drug mules, cartel leaders can ensure a successful smuggling operation by bribing customs officials and airport security screeners to ignore their drug shipments. According to federal authorities, some cartels have even worked to plant their own people in the Transportation Security Administration (TSA), the government agency that oversees airport security checks and baggage handlers. The relatively small amounts of contraband carried by drug mules that trickles through the system every day adds up to a highly profitable operation.

Alliances with American Gangs

Once drugs have arrived in the United States, they must be distributed to customers. To make this happen, the major drug cartels have made alliances with street gangs in the United States. Gang members work for the cartels as smugglers and as foot soldiers, defending shipments and threatening or eliminating anyone who would interfere with the cartel's activities. In exchange, they receive the right to distribute the cartel's drugs and profit from drug sales throughout the nation.

Historically, street gangs have been formed by people with a shared racial or ethnic background, and the gangs traditionally fought bitter wars with gangs made up of people with different racial or ethnic characteristics. At one time, for example, it would have been unthinkable for a violent gang like the

 Did You Know?

A gang known as Mara Salvatrucha or MS-13, is one of the most violent and dangerous gangs in the United States. MS-13 originated in Los Angeles, and was made up of people from El Salvador. The gang's motto—*mata, roba, viola, controla* ("kill, steal, rape, control")— expresses its ruthlessness. MS-13 has spread beyond Los Angeles, and currently works with drug cartels as assassins or smugglers.

Immigration and Customs Enforcement (ICE) agents arrest a Mexican gang member involved in drug trafficking.

Aryan Brotherhood, which believes that white people are superior to all other races, to work together with Mexican drug cartels or gangs made up of Hispanics or African Americans. However, the huge profits to be made from drug dealing have led gangs to suspend their traditional ideologies in order to make money.

Street gangs in the border states like Texas, New Mexico, Arizona, and California are responsible for the distribution of drugs in Los Angeles and other western U.S. cities. They also move drugs across the country, making arrangements with gangs in the Midwest and on the East Coast to carry on the trade nationally. Such gangs include the infamous Bloods and Crips of Los Angeles, as well as Mara Salvatrucha, the Mexican Mafia, and many others.

 Text-Dependent Questions

1. How much funding does the U.S. Congress provide for the Drug Enforcement Administration (DEA) each year?
2. What has happened to the street price of heroin over the past twenty-five years?
3. What are some creative ways that cartels are able to smuggle their drugs from Mexico into the United States?
4. What is a "drug mule?"

 Research Project

Visit the National Institute on Drug Abuse's Emerging Trends and Alerts webpage at https://www.drugabuse.gov/drugs-abuse/emerging-trends-alerts. Scroll down to the alerts, located in boxes with an exclamation point icon in the corner. Choose one of the alerts and write a one-page essay summarizing the issue.

 Words to Understand in This Chapter

dependency—a condition in which a person cannot function without the use of something, such as drugs.

mandatory minimum sentences—the requirement that a person convicted of a crime must be imprisoned for a specific, predetermined period, as opposed to leaving the duration of imprisonment up to the judge.

quota—a limit on the amount of something.

5

Young people participate in a group therapy session with an addiction counselor. As understanding of the scope of the heroin crisis has grown, communities have begun making more drug rehabilitation programs available to those who become addicted.

What Can Be Done?

The first step to solving any problem is to admit that the problem exists. American medical providers and law-enforcement officials have recognized for several years that the U.S. is in the midst of a heroin crisis. In fact, some have said that the heroin crisis one of the most severe public health problems in the nation's history.

The government has taken steps to try to reduce the availability of illegal drugs like heroin, as well as prescription opioids like fentanyl. For many years, authorities preferred a zero-tolerance approach. State and federal laws like the 1986 Anti-Drug Abuse Act established *mandatory minimum sentences* for people convicted of selling heroin or other drugs like marijuana, cocaine, or methamphetamine. Under this law, the first time a federal court convicts a person of dealing one of these

49

drugs, the person must serve a prison sentence of at least five years. The sentence could be even higher, depending on the quantity of the drug sold and whether violence was involved. A second conviction for selling drugs includes a mandatory sentence of at least ten years, and possibly as much as a life term behind bars.

However, many people have come to believe these mandatory penalties are much too harsh. Critics of mandatory minimum sentencing laws point out that a first-time offender who sells a few hundred dollars worth of drugs faces the same penalty that the boss of a drug cartel would receive if convicted.

Another issue is that these laws have resulted in a huge increase in the U.S. prison population since the mid-1980s. In 1980, the U.S. had about 330,000 prison inmates—roughly 150 prison inmates for every 100,000 citizens. By 2017, the number of inmates had risen to over 2.3 million, and the incarceration rate was nearly five times higher than in 1980, at about 700 inmates per 100,000 citizens. Much of the increase in prison population is due to the war on drugs and the mandatory prison sentences for people convicted of drug-related offenses. Today, about 20 percent of all prison inmates have been convicted of using or selling drugs.

Also, there is evidence that the arrests of drug users and deals has no effect on the operations of drug cartels. Drug lords quickly assign new dealers and smugglers to replace those who are caught by police. Even higher-ranking officials of the cartel can be easily replaced. Unless police are able to capture the cartel's leader and destroy its infrastructure, the drugs continue to flow freely.

According to the US Department of Justice, which oversees the federal prison system, approximately half of all inmates in federal prisons are serving time for drug-related offenses. In state prisons, more than 200,000 inmates are incarcerated on drug charges as of 2017. This is roughly 16 percent of the total population of the state prison systems.

Drug Treatment Programs

Perhaps one of the biggest differences in the current heroin crisis is the demographics of the users. At one time, heroin users were likely to be poor whites, African Americans, or Hispanics. They were the stereotypical "junkies" who lived outside of the mainstream society and were primarily concerned about getting their next "fix" of hard drugs to stave off the symptoms of withdrawal.

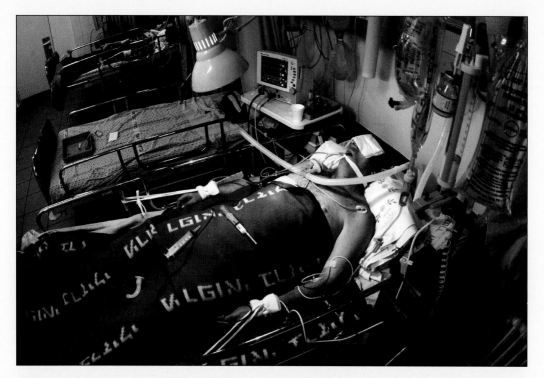

In the most severe cases of drug addiction, patients might need to rid their bodies of the drug in a hospital setting. Rapid opioid detoxification treatment is considered to be an effective method of getting people off drugs in the short term.

The current heroin epidemic has resulted in a major change in the demographics of drug users. Today, heroin addicts are more likely to be white and middle class than ever before. The number of women who are addicted to heroin is growing. As the profile of the typical heroin user has shifted, many people have encouraged a "kinder" war against drugs that replaces incarceration with rehabilitation programs.

Heroin addicts can stop taking drugs with the help of special treatment programs. Until the 1970s, the only way for most people to end their drug abuse was simply to stop taking the drugs. This was often very unpleasant in the case of hero-in, due to the strong withdrawal symptoms that can last for several weeks. Today, there are alternatives for those looking to kick their habit.

If users want to stop taking heroin, a doctor may offer them a synthetic medicine called methadone. This opioid drug pro-duces feelings similar to those produced by heroin, but it is not as strong or addictive. Addicts sometimes find it is a step towards giving up their *dependency* on heroin. Unfortunately, methadone also has side effects, which are similar to those of the drug it replaces. If too much methadone is taken, it can result in a fatal overdose.

People who want to stop taking drugs often find it helps them to talk to a professional counselor. They can talk about why they took drugs in the first place, how to cope with with-drawal symptoms, and life after drugs. Sometimes, drug users are also placed in rehabilitation programs. These can provide a safe place for a few days or weeks, where there are no illegal drugs and there is plenty of counselling available. Courts have the option of sending convicted drug offenders into rehabilita-tion programs.

 Educational Video

To understand why it is so hard to quit drugs, scan here:

Did You Know?

In March 2017, China banned the legal manufacture and sale of several variations of fentanyl—carfentanil, furanyl fentanyl, acrylfentanyl, and valeryl fentanyl. The ban was implemented after six months of talks between American and Chinese officials about the heroin and opioid crisis. American officials praised the decision because China is the leading supplier of fentanyl to the United States.

Rehabilitation is considered an extremely useful tool for breaking the cycle of drug dependence. In 2016, the Office of National Drug Control Policy spent about 43 percent of its annual budget—over $13.4 billion—on drug treatment programs.

According to the annual National Survey on Drug Use and Health, conducted by the Substance Abuse and Mental Health Services Administration (SAMHSA), there is a large "treatment gap" in the United States. In 2014, the most recent year for which data is available, an estimated 22.7 million Americans (8.6 percent of the total population) needed treatment for a problem related to drugs or alcohol. However, only about 2.5 million people (0.9 percent) received treatment at a specialty facility.

Education and Prevention

Government officials and medical professionals agree that one way to end the heroin crisis is to educate people about the dangers of opioid painkillers, and reduce the number of people who become addicted to them. The government has also begun providing educational training and resources to healthcare providers so they can make better decisions when it comes to prescribing opioid painkillers.

Reducing the supply of opioids is another way to address the problem. In October 2016, the DEA announced that it would reduce the production *quota* for oxycodone, hydrocodone, fentanyl, and morphine by at least 25 percent in an attempt to curb the epidemic.

Electronic databases can make it easier for doctors and pharmacists to track the past drug histories of patients before they receive prescriptions for opioid painkillers. This would reduce the number of people who obtain pills illegally by visiting multiple doctors.

Scene from inside a heroin-processing facility that was busted by DEA agents in 2017. This table is covered with small packets of heroin, which each sell for about $30. According to a 2014 Pew Research Center study, 26 percent of Americans want the government to focus more on prosecuting illegal drug users, while 67 percent of them want the government to focus more on providing treatment for illegal drug users.

The federal government has also proposed that prescription drug monitoring programs—electronic databases that track the dispensing of certain drugs—should become a routine part of clinical practice. This way doctors or pharmacists could analyze a patient's prescription drug history before prescribing opioid painkillers. Health care providers should ask their patients about past or current drug and alcohol use before they consider opioid treatment. If they do decide to prescribe an opioid, it should be the lowest effective dose, and only the quantity needed for the patient.

As the dangerous side effects of opioids become better known, pharmaceutical companies are working on developing pain medications that are less prone to abuse. One drug being studied by a pair of researchers from Duke University addresses different nerve receptors than opioids do, providing painkilling benefits without the dangerous side effects. Several other drugs are in development that could replace opioids in the future.

 Text-Dependent Questions

1. What are mandatory minimum sentences?
2. How do treatment programs help heroin addicts?
3. What are prescription drug monitoring programs?

 Research Project

By contacting local law enforcement and criminal justice agencies, or by accessing information available on websites and in official publications, ask about the use of drug courts in your state or province. If they are not available in your area, ask about programs designed to keep offenders off drugs and out of prisons. Write several paragraphs about your findings.

Series Glossary

analgesic—any member of a class of drugs used to achieve analgesia, or relief from pain.

central nervous system—the part of the human nervous system that consists of the brain and spinal cord. These are greatly affected by opiates and opioids.

dependence—a situation that occurs when opiates or opioids are used so much that the user's body adapts to the drug and only functions normally when the drug is present. When the user attempts to stop using the drug, a physiologic reaction known as withdrawal syndrome occurs.

epidemic—a widespread occurrence of a disease or illness in a community at a particular time.

opiates—a drug that is derived directly from the poppy plant, such as opium, heroin, morphine, and codeine.

opioids—synthetic drugs that affect the body in a similar way as opiate drugs. The opioids include Oxycotin, hydrocodone, fentanyl, and methadone.

withdrawal—a syndrome of often painful physical and psychological symptoms that occurs when someone stops using an addictive drug, such as an opiate or opioid. Often, the drug user will begin taking the drug again to avoid withdrawal.

Further Reading

Gammill, Joani. *Painkillers, Heroin, and the Road to Sanity*. Center City, MN: Hazelden, 2014.

Hari, Johann. *Chasing the Scream: The First and Last Days of the War on Drugs*. New York: Bloomsbury, 2015.

Horning, Nicole. *Heroin: Killer Drug Epidemic*. San Diego: Lucent Books, 2017.

Quinones, Sam. *Dreamland: The True Tale of America's Opiate Epidemic*. New York: Bloomsbury Press, 2015.

Sanna, E.J. *Heroin and Other Opioids*. Philadelphia: Mason Crest, 2012.

Sheff, David. *Clean: Overcoming Addiction and Ending America's Greatest Tragedy*. New York: Houghton Mifflin Harcourt, 2013.

Internet Resources

www.dea.gov/druginfo/factsheets.shtml

The Drug Enforcement Administration (DEA) maintains fact sheets on opiates like heroin, opioids like oxycodone, and other drugs of concern.

https://easyread.drugabuse.gov/

The National Institute on Drug Abuse maintains a webpage called Easy-to-Read Drug Facts that contains short videos, drug profiles, and personal stories of teens in recovery.

www.cdc.gov/drugoverdose/prescribing/patients.html

The CDC maintains a webpage with helpful information about opioids and the dangers associated with them.

www.drugfreeworld.org/real-life-stories/heroin.html

The Foundation for a Drug-Free World provides a video and real life quotes from heroin addicts.

Publisher's Note: The websites listed on these pages were active at the time of publication. The publisher is not responsible for websites that have changed their address or discontinued operation since the date of publication. The publisher reviews and updates the websites each time the book is reprinted.

www.drugabuse.gov/drugs-abuse/opioids

The website of the National Institute on Drug Abuse includes statistics related to the opioid epidemic, as well as articles and drug information.

www.ccsa.ca

This website delivers a wide range of publications on substance abuse in Canada. Subjects relate to prescription drugs and alcohol, drug treatment, impaired driving, abuse prevention, and other drug-related topics.

www.samhsa.gov

A vast amount of research related to opioids and other substances can be performed on the Substance Abuse and Mental Health Services Administration website. The website also provides resources on national strategies and initiatives, state and local initiatives, and training and education.

www.nar-anon.org/

Nar-Anon is a 12-step program for the families and friends of addicts with meetings all over the world.

Index

Numbers in ***bold italic*** refer to captions.

About the Author

John Cashin is the author of several books for young adults. He has written about current events for a number of print and online publications. A graduate of Penn State University, he lives near Philadelphia.

Picture Credits: DEA Photo: 6, 8, 22, 26, 28 (right), 30, 38, 40, 43, 56; Everett Collection: 16, 19; © OTTN Publishing: 11; used under license from Shutterstock, Inc.: 1, 2, 14, 28 (left), 48, 51, 52, 55; Photoshooter2015 / Shutterstock.com: 34; U.S. Department of Homeland Security Immigration and Customs Enforcement (ICE) photo: 44, 46.